# Ella's Stories

*Lillie Mae Jordan and Mary Kathleen Preston*

Copyright © 2021 by Lillie Mae Jordan and Mary Kathleen Preston

All rights reserved. No part of this publication may be reproduced, distributed, or transmitted in any form or by any means, including photocopying, recording, or other electronic or mechanical methods, without the prior written permission of the publisher, except in the case brief quotations embodied in critical reviews and other noncommercial uses permitted by copyright law.

ISBN:   978-1-954341-28-9 (Paperback)

The views expressed in this book are solely those of the author and do not necessarily reflect the views of the publisher, and the publisher hereby disclaims any responsibility for them.

Writers' Branding
1800-608-6550
www.writersbranding.com
orders@writersbranding.com

# Contents

Dedication Page . . . . . . . . . . . . . . . . . . . . . . . . . . . . . . . . . . . . 1
Ella's big adventure . . . . . . . . . . . . . . . . . . . . . . . . . . . . . . . . . 3
Ella's Birthday . . . . . . . . . . . . . . . . . . . . . . . . . . . . . . . . . . . . . 7
Ella and the sleigh bells . . . . . . . . . . . . . . . . . . . . . . . . . . . . . 13
The forest fire that almost came . . . . . . . . . . . . . . . . . . . . . . 17
Ella starts school . . . . . . . . . . . . . . . . . . . . . . . . . . . . . . . . . . 23
Ella's Christmas surprise . . . . . . . . . . . . . . . . . . . . . . . . . . . 27
Yum Yum . . . . . . . . . . . . . . . . . . . . . . . . . . . . . . . . . . . . . . . 31
Ella Goes away to school . . . . . . . . . . . . . . . . . . . . . . . . . . . 33
Alex's Christmas Surprise . . . . . . . . . . . . . . . . . . . . . . . . . . 41
The Journey . . . . . . . . . . . . . . . . . . . . . . . . . . . . . . . . . . . . . 43

# Dedication Page

These are stories that Ella told to her two little girls, after she was grown. The girls preferred them to fairy tales at bedtime. They are accurate to the best of my memory. I am the older of the two girls. I am Mary Kathleen.

During the hardest years of my life after my son was killed in an accident, and my husband had a heart attack, I was able to cling to these stories and remember the better times in my childhood on Grandfathers' farm. They meant so much to me that I told them to my grandchildren who loved them as much as I did. I would like to share them with you. May you be blessed with the rich history of our young nation in the early 1900's.

Christmas and the Journey are Ella's parents Alex's and Mary's stories as told by Grandpa Alex himself.

Mary Kathleen spent one month each summer of her childhood on grandfathers' Dairy farm. Grandfather told her stories of his life in Scotland and the move to America. It is truly amazing what the immigrants were willing to face to make a move to this amazing country of America. We sometimes forget the stories, but I believe the strength and ingenuity of these fine people are important stories in our history and should be passed down from one family member to another, one generation to another. Prayer was a big part of my grandparents' life and legacy. Even when I was a child grandfather read a chapter out of the Old Testament and a chapter of the New Testament each evening.

May the peace of living on the farm abound in your heart, as you read these stories.

*Ella's Stories*

This book is dedicated to my granddaughters and Ella's great granddaughters Melissa, Kendra, Amanda, Joanna and Nicole, and the entire Bews family, with much love. Grandmother Mary Kathleen.

Back row left to right: John Harry, Alexander, Mary Jane  Middle row: Mary Harray Bews, Rosemund Miller (beloved neighbor) Front row: Eddie, Eleanor

# Ella's big adventure

"Everything is packed in the wagon and ready to go'" said Father. "The tent is packed, the food is packed, extra clothes and blankets are packed." Everyone was getting excited and looking forward to the long trip to Salem, they were going to pick hops to earn money for the mortgage payment on the farm.

Father had bought the farm the year before but didn't have quite enough money to pay off the mortgage all at one time. The family was hopeful that they could pay off the mortgage this year.

As they traveled along the bumpy dirt road, they sang songs and told stories to entertain themselves. The sun was hot, and they were getting awfully tired. When evening came, they were all very glad to stop and lay out their bedding on the ground and build a campfire and cook some supper. There was no need to put up that big old tent for only one night.

Everyone was glad when they finally got to Salem, the next day, and found the field where they were going to pick hops. They found a good place to set up their tent. This was going to be their home for two whole weeks while they worked.

The next morning, they were up early. They ate their breakfast and started out to the field to pick. "Ella", said father, "you are big enough to help us this year. Remember they pay us a penny a pound for the hops we pick. You are tall enough to pick all the lower ones and mother and I can get the top ones."

Father put her name on the list of pickers and the field boss gave her a big LONG gunny sack, of burlap, to fill with hops. It looked verrrry big, but she wanted to try anyway.

Father showed her how to pull the hops off the vines and put them in her bag, then drag the bag along behind her.

Ella began to pick. There were lots and lots of hops to pull off the vines. The day grew warmer and she got tired. After lunch, Father put little brother Eddie, on a soft pile of empty gunny sacks for a nap. Then he said, "Ella", you look tired, why don't you come and lie down too. I'll pick your part of the row while you sleep."

Ella laid down and found the pile of sacks very comfortable. She could hear a bee buzzing somewhere nearby. The shade under the hops plants was cool and welcome and she was asleep in no time.

Each day went by the same as the one before it. Soon their two weeks were finished. The fields were picked clean of hops. It was time to collect their money and go home. Ella remembered the hops were one penny a pound so she expected a whole lot of pennies for all of her hard work. More than she could hold in both hands.

Everyone got in line in front of the table that the field boss had set up for his records. Each bag of hops had been weighed on a scale and the weight was written down next to the name of the person who picked it. Now, as each person gave him their name, he added up how many pounds of hops they had picked and paid them the amount of money they had earned.

When Ella stepped up to the table and told her name, the field boss said "well young lady, you did a good job of picking hops. You picked two hundred pounds of hops, so you earned twenty dollars." Then he gave her one small coin, a twenty-dollar gold piece, but to little Ella, it was just one small coin and she imagined that she had earned stacks and stacks of pennies, nickles and dimes. She said, "Thank you very much!" to the field boss, but in her heart, she was very disappointed. SHE HAD WORKED SO VERY HARD FOR SO LONG.

She didn't know what to do with the gold coin, so she gave it to her father. He saw how disappointed she was, "Ella, he said, you know that Mother and I need all the money to make the payment on our land. If you are willing for me to use your twenty dollars, I will sell you twenty dollars' worth of our land and you can pick out any piece you want. When we get home, I'll sit down and figure out how many square feet it will be. Would that be all right?" "And it would be my very own?" asked Ella. "Yes" replied Father, "to keep as long as we have the farm."

"Oh, goodie" giggled Ella. "I'd like that!"

When they finally arrived at home, Ella went out in the yard to pick her special place. She chose one of her favorite places…Mother's garden. Her Father measured out the right amount of land and built a fence around it for her!

When Father was too old to work his farm any longer, he asked his son, Eddie and wife Pauline, to move back to the family farm from Idaho, and he gave the farm to Ella's younger brother Eddie who worked it for over 30 years. Grandfather Alex lived in the old log cabin until he passed away.

Grandfather used to get his oats from the cow feed the night before and soak them in water before cooking them in the morning. He always said that the cows' oats tasted better than the oats he could buy at the grocery store. Grandfather would make oatmeal with fresh cream each morning and feed a bowl to his favorite chicken Biddie, who would come to the log house for breakfast. (this chicken lived 10 or more years and loved grandfather.

When Ed and his wife decided to move to George Washington in 1962, and sold the farm, the sum of five thousand dollars was paid to

*Ella's Stories*

Ella for her share of mother's garden, that she had worked for so very long ago when she was a small child.

# Ella's Birthday.

It was a bright morning in January. Ella woke up early, she ran to the window and looked out. Everything still looked like Winter, but it seemed different today. "Today is my Birthday", she thought. "It's my birthday ALL DAY LONG".

She hurried and got dressed, tied two blue ribbons to the end of her red braids. Then ran downstairs to breakfast.

"Mother, Mother", she said, "its' such a beautiful day!" "Good morning" her mother said, "and Happy Birthday, Ella!" "Happy Birthday, Ella" said her father. "Happy Birthday", said her sister Mary and her brothers John and Eddie. It's Saturday and we don't have to go to school, but we still have chores to do, so eat your breakfast" said Mary.

They lived on a farm and there were always chickens and pigs to feed, cows to milk and lots of other things to do down at the barn. Ella was just glad that there wasn't any snow on the ground because that always made more work with the animals.

Then mother said "Ella, since today is your birthday, we have thought of a special gift for you. Since there is no school today, we want you to do anything you want to do. No one will be able to tell you "no" or "stop doing that". You don't have to do chores if you don't want to. You can play or sing or go for a walk or anything else you want to do."

Now this is a special treat for any little girl who lives on a dairy farm because there is always work for everyone to do.

Ella said, "Oh! Thank you, thank you very much mother", and finished her oatmeal. "Can I really do anything I want to?" "Yes dear, you can. Please just keep yourself safe." "I will mother, I promise, said Ella as she finished her glass of milk. "May I go now and start on my birthday?" "Of course, dear," said mother.

"What will you do first?" "Oh mother, there are so many things, I can't decide," said Ella. "Maybe I should just sit and think."

Ella sat down on the front steps to think. "I've always wondered what was under the front steps," she thought. "Maybe I should see," so she crawled under the steps. There were cobwebs and sow bugs and earwigs, but there was plenty of room to lay on her stomach. "Well, she thought, now I know."

*Ella's Stories*

She took a walk down to the barn to visit the animals. The horses and cows had been turned out to pasture. The farm cat was busy chasing a small grey mouse and didn't pay any attention to her. It was too early in the year for baby calves, pigs or kittens." There's nothing to do here," she thought, so she went out to the orchard.

It was wintertime and the trees were bare. There wasn't much to do but climb trees. Ella soon tired of that, so she decided to check out the blacksmith shed. Much to her delight, her father was there, building up the fire and getting ready to shoe the work horses.

Ella loved to watch him work. She loved to watch him heat up the shoes, pound them into shape and put them on the horses. After he got the fire going, he tied the first horse to a tree close by and pulled out the old nails, took off the old worn out shoes, one at a time. Then he filed each hoof just so and fit a new shoe to it. He would heat the shoe until it was red and pound it on his anvil until it was just the same shape as the hoof and then put it on with special horseshoe nails. When he had finished the second horse, he spread the charcoal so the fire would go out and we went into the house for our noon meal.

After they finished their meat, potatoes and vegetables, mother brought out a big birthday cake with candles on it. Everyone sang happy birthday to Ella then she helped her mom cut a big piece of the cake for each member of the family. It tasted so good. Mother always said that birthday cake tastes better than every-day cakes, no matter what flavor they were.

When they were all through eating, Mary helped mother clear away the dishes and wash them. This was usually Ella's job! But it was her birthday and she didn't have to do them. Ella went into the bedroom that she shared with her sister Mary and got out her paper dolls, she examined them carefully and decided they needed birthday dresses for her birthday. Ella got out some paper, a pencil, crayons and scissors and drew them lovely, fancy dresses for each paper doll. She colored each one a different color and carefully cut them out. When she was done with her paper-dolls she took a nap.

Mother woke her up to come to the kitchen table for some supper. Since it was still her birthday, her father gave her a little extra cream on her corn flakes.

After supper was cleared away and Ella was crawling into bed, she said, "you know, mother, this has been my best birthday yet!"

# Ella and the sleigh bells

It was Winter time. The sun was just coming up when Ella opened her eyes. It was Sunday morning and the whole family was going to church. A minister was coming out from town today, just to preach at their little church and he was coming to Ella's house for dinner. Mother had spent most of Saturday baking pies and bread just for today's dinner. (the little church was just big enough for 4 families with four pews and room for 4 adults in each pew)

Ella hopped out of bed and ran to close her bedroom window. As she looked out… her heart sank! "Oh, no!" she cried. "It snowed last night. It snowed a lot!" Everything was white and fluffy looking and sparkling in the early morning sunshine. She hurried to put on her clothes and started downstairs for breakfast.

When she saw her father, she said, "Daddy, Daddy, what are we going to do? It snowed last night and it's too deep to get to church."

"You're right," said father. "We haven't had this much snow in several years, but you are forgetting something." His eyes twinkled. "Sit down and eat your breakfast. I will be right back with our ride to church."

*Ella's Stories*

Father went out the back door and headed for the barn as Ella sat down to a steaming bowl of oatmeal. Her sister Mary and brothers John and Eddie were already eating. Mother put her hand on Ella's shoulder and said "don't worry about getting to church.

Just remember… "where there is a will, there is a way,"

Ella was not sure just what that meant but kept on eating anyway. Just as she was taking her last spoonful of oatmeal from her bowl, she began to hear a jingling sound. It came closer and closer.

Why it sounded like those little brass jingling bells on that old leather harness that hung on a post out in the barn. They all ran to the front window to see what it was.

"Mother, Mother" cried Ella, "come and see." Sure enough there were the brass jingle bells and the old leather harness- on the horse- hitched up to the sleigh that father kept under the canvass in the corner of the barn And the sleigh rode just fine on top of all that puffy white snow.

"This will be fun, said mother." Put on your coats, I have comforters for our laps.

## "WE ARE GOING TO CHURCH!"

**Dover Church**

(The sleigh was a converted hay wagon with the wheels taken off and the runners installed. The runners were kept in the barn under canvas when not in use.)

John, Mary, Ella and Eddie Bews were the children of Scottish immigrants and were born just at the turn of the century, Eddie the youngest was born in 1901. They lived with their parents on a homestead near Mt Hood, Oregon.

# The forest fire that almost came

Ella was sitting at the dinner table with her brothers John, Eddie and her sister Mary. Father had just finished eating and Mother was drinking her cup of tea. "There certainly was a lot of smoke in the air this morning", said Father. "Either someone is burning a large brush pile or there is a forest fire near-by." Just then, there was a loud knock at the door and father answered it. It was their neighbor down the road. "Alex", he began. "we need you and your fine son. There's forest fire started up on Mt. Hood and the wind is blowing it this way. Better grab your team and wagon with some supplies and follow my son and me. Other neighbors are heading up that way, too."

Father looked worried. Their new house was built of wood and so was their barn. If the wind blew just right, it could burn their place to the ground. "Mother," he said quietly, "I'll go ---."

"May I come too--- please?" asked John.

"Yes," said father. "We will take the smaller wagon and leave you the hay wagon, Mother. You and Mary will have to hitch it up and load it in case you have to leave our home in a hurry!"

"Don't worry about us!" said mother." "We'll be fine," "I'll get some food ready for you to take, while you get your other supplies." "All right," said Father. "John please hitch up the team."

John hurriedly left the table and headed for the barn and the horses. After all, he was almost twelve years old now and knew how to hitch the wagon and even knew how to drive it. He liked animals, especially horses and this was a good team who would obediently take them to the scene of the fire.

By the time John drove the wagon up to the house father had a pile of blankets, clothes, containers of water, food, shovels and other necessities piled in the front yard. John was glad he had remembered to put in half a sack of oats for the horses. They would get hungry too.

John and his father quickly left and followed their neighbors down the road and into the smoke.

"Now you three have to help me," said mother. "I promised your father we would stay safe. Let me tell you our plan. The fire could come this way, so we must be prepared. We want to save as much food as we can, our beds, and some clothes. You know that we have our root cellar and how it is built underground, which will keep it from burning even if the house does.

Mary, will you start by carrying our canned fruit, and vegetables down into the root cellar, but please save out a dozen or so jars to take on the wagon with us. Then we will put a change of clothes for each of us in the root cellar and some blankets in the wagon. Please get started while I go hitch up the hay wagon.

Ella, it will be your job to look out for Baby Eddie. He is apt to get frightened and cry, so you will have to be very brave and keep him happy."

Mother headed for the barn and the second team of horses. They were Morgans, a large breed of horses and that were used to plow the farm. Mary Bew was a very small woman, less than 5 feet tall, but the horses were patient and gentle and in no time at all she had the big old hay wagon hitched and the patient animals headed for the house. Mother tied the reins to the gate post and went into the house to get things to load into the wagon."

"Children," she called. "We won't have to leave unless we can see the fire in the forest behind the house, but we need to be loaded and ready to go at a moment's notice.

As soon as we are loaded, I think we should do some extra baking, so we have enough for a several days. We also need a lookout to watch for signs of the fire coming."

"Eddie and I can watch for the fire while we pay in the yard," offered Ella. "All right," replied mother. "Mary and I can do the baking. While we are at it, we will think up something for supper since we are home alone. After that we will take turns on fire watch. That will be a very important job."

Ella felt very important. It wasn't every day that a six- year- old was trusteed with two such jobs at once. Eddie was being very good and stayed very close to his sister and didn't give her any trouble. They didn't find playing very much fun. They were too interested in watching for signs of the fire.

Mother and Mary fixed some wonderful soup and corn bread for supper, but they all found they were a little too worried to eat very much.

Mary took over the job of watching for the fire after they ate, and mother put Eddie to sleep downstairs in her own bed. It seemed very strange to have Father and John gone for the night, but they had taken blankets with them along with food and water, so they would be fine. They could sleep in the wagon they had brought with them.

When the three children were in bed, Mother took over the fire watch. In the middle of the night she woke Mary to take over the watch so she could sleep. Mother knew she had to keep up her strength. She got up early the next morning and took over the watch for Mary. Mary was only ten years old and Mother didn't want to ask too much of her.

The smoke was thicker that it had been the day before. They could barely see an orange glow where the sun was. The wind was still blowing toward them and Mary Bews was worried about her children, her husband and their home. She prayed that God would keep them all safe.

The heavy smoky day dragged on and into the second night. They continued to watch for the fire. Mother and Mary were both very tired but too nervous to sleep. The patient horses were still tied to the gate post. They had been fed hay and oats and had water in the big buckets. They had been petted and talked to and the gentle giants seemed to understand that they must stand and wait to be ready to go.

The horses didn't like the smell of smoke or the feel of it in their eyes, but they waited.

Time continued to drag slowly by. The little family wondered about their father and brother and where the fire was today.

Ella carried her favorite doll with her so that there was no chance that she would be left behind. She watched out for Eddie and took her daytime turn watching the forest for signs of the fire.

On the morning of the fifth day, they saw what they had been dreading--red flames beginning to show in the forest and the wind was still blowing it toward them.

"Come children," said Mother quietly. "I think it is time to go." They made sure that the root cellar lid was shut tight and the windows closed in the house, the fire was out in the kitchen stove and the front door was latched.

Mother put little Eddie in the pile of blankets in the back of the wagon. Ella sat down beside him. Mary sat next to Ella, and Mother started to get up on the seat to drive.

"Does the air seem fresher?" asked Mother. "Look, I think the wind is changing." They all sat and watched. The wind was changing, in fact it was blowing the smoky red forest fire back away from them.

They sat for quite a while, until they were sure the fire wasn't coming any more. It wasn't burning so hard. It was being blown back into the area that had already burned and so there was no fuel for the fire, and it died out after a while.

As soon as they were sure it was safe, Mother, Mary, Ella and little Eddie unloaded the wagon. They were very thankful that they hadn't had to use it to escape from the blazing fire.

Mother took the wagon and team of patient horses back to the barn. She took off their harness and put each horse in its own stall and gave it a bunch of hay and some oats. Then she and the children set about to cook a big hot dinner. They made a big pot roast with potatoes and carrots, fresh bread with real butter and a big apple pie.

Sure enough, in the late afternoon, they could see a wagon coming down the road, pulled by two very tired and very sooty horses and two men riding in it who were all dirty and hard to recognize. They pulled into the yard. It was Father and John.

We're home! " they called, but it wasn't necessary because their family was outside waiting for them.

After many hugs and kisses, Father said, "let's unload this wagon so I can take these good animals to the barn and feed them."

Father drew some water from the well and put it in their water trough. As soon as they finished drinking, he took them to the barn, and put them in their stalls where he fed them fresh hay and an extra handful of oats. "I'll come down in the morning and brush you well, but I must see about my family first," he told them.

Father went back to the house and found that Mother had heated water and had a hot bath waiting for him.

After they had eaten their fill of pot roast, vegetables, bread with real butter and apple pie (Father's very favorite meal). Father said thoughtfully, "you know, it was strange the way the wind changed today. It blew the fire back onto itself and burned it out.

There are still some spots that are hot, but I think it is going to be safe. It was almost like God had blown on it– like answered prayer!"

The next few days Father checked the damage from the fire and found that there was no damage to their homestead. The fire turned around at the fence line and blew back onto itself. What a blessing Father received for being a man of God.

# Ella starts school

It was a warm and lazy day in the summer. The sun was shining, the corn in the garden was as tall as Ella and the beautiful Brown Swiss cows were standing in the shade of the barn, swishing their tails to keep the flies off.

Ella felt bored. She wanted something different to do. The noon meal was finished, and the dishes were washed and put away.

"Ella," said mother as she set out the fresh bread out of the oven and on to cooling racks. "I think it's time we started thinking about school this fall."

"School, already?" questioned Ella. "But mother, it is still summer."

"I know, dear, but fall will be here before you know it. It takes time to get things out of the big catalogue."

"Oh, goodie," cried Ella as she ran to get the big catalogue off the bookshelf above the old chest in the living room.

"Bring it to the table, dear, so we can both see it," said mother. Ella began turning the pages in the front of the open catalogue. "Find the shoes first, said mother. "then we will need to find some good wool fabric for a new dress."

Ella turned pages and pages until she came to the shoes. There were all sizes of shoes. Most of them were high topped with buttons up the sides. Some were low heels and some had high heels. Some were brown and some were black.

Mother read the descriptions and found a pair that were for girls Ella's age. "I think this will do nicely," said Mother. "Now we have to measure your foot to see what size to order," said Mother. Mother took a big piece of butcher paper and a pencil and had Ella put her bare

## Ella's Stories

foot right in the middle. Then she drew exactly around her foot with a pencil. "Now", mother said, we can match this up with the chart in the catalogue and see what size you are now. Then we will order a size bigger, no—maybe two sizes bigger, since you are growing so fast, so they will still fit you this winter."

"Oh, Mother, said Ella, I can hardly wait. New leather shoes always smell so good and I feel so dressed up when I wear them. Mother? "May I have a brown dress to go with my brown shoes?" Ella sked?

"Let's look at the fabric samples and see," said Mother, as she turned some more pages to find the fabric section of the catalogue. "Mrs. Thomas is coming next month to sew for us, and I want to get everything ready first."

They looked at the fabric in the catalog and picked out a piece of pretty brown, light weight wool fabric with sewing thread and buttons to match. Mother filled out the order for Ella and added shoes and other things for the rest of the family.

Then Mother got out the jar of "egg money" that was earned from selling butter and eggs from the farm and took out the amount that was needed to pay for the items.

Ella was anxious for the catalogue order to arrive and at the same time, she didn't want the warm days of summer to end. But time passed quickly, and it seemed no time at all until the catalogue order arrived, and just in time, too. The very next day, Mrs. Thomas was to arrive to spend the week with them to do the school sewing.

Mother had a beautiful sewing machine in a fine oak cabinet with roses carved on it and a box lid that set over the top. Mrs. Thomas came each fall and sewed for Mother and Mother paid her from the butter and egg money.

*Ella's Stories*

When Mrs. Thomas came, she measured Ella and then laid out her patterns on the pretty brown fabric and started cutting. By the end of the day, she had almost finished Ella's new dress.

Ella just couldn't wait to try it on. It was just perfect. Then she tried on her shoes. The matched her dress just fine, but they were very big on her feet. Mother leaned over and felt her toes. "I know how to fix this.", said Mother. She took some brown butcher paper and crumpled it. Took off Ell's new shoes and fit the crumpled paper in the toes. "there now, try that on and see if it's any better?" she said. Ella said, "and I'll still be able to wear them next spring."

Ella's face beamed with delight as she said, "thank you, Mother." Now I'm all-ready for school to start." "I can't wait for my first day of school."

# Ella's Christmas surprise

It was a quiet Saturday afternoon. It was cold and rainy outside and Ella was playing with her dolls beside the kitchen stove. She had made a cozy bed for them out of an apple box. There was a little tiny doll with a red gingham dress, a slightly larger one in a blue nightshirt and a corn husk doll that wasn't very cuddly. They had been good and faithful dolls, as long as Ella could remember, but she really wanted a doll that she could rock and cuddle like a real child. "Mother," said Ella, "is Christmas coming pretty soon?"

Corn Husk Doll

"Christmas" questioned her mother, "yes, I believe it is just over a month away. "Why would you want to know?" "Well", said Ella,

"I was just thinking about how nice it would be to have a new dolly, maybe, for Christmas." "A doll for Christmas," said mother, "that would be fun, wouldn't it? Well, you never know what will come." Her mother's eyes twinkled but Ella didn't notice.

Day after Day passed by, Ella didn't mention Christmas again, but she was still thinking about a new doll. One night after Ella and her sister were both asleep, Ella woke up and was feeling thirsty, decided to go quietly downstairs for a drink of water. There was an oil lamp lit in the living room and she decided to see who was still up.

She stood on the stairs and peeked around the corner, there sat Mother in her rocking chair next to the table with the oil lamp on it. She was surrounded by bits of cloth and some pieces of something she seemed to be sewing. Ella stood very still and quiet. She continued to watch, fascinated by what Mother was doing. Suddenly, she realized what mother was making— a rag doll! A beautiful Christmas rag doll!

Ella forgot all about the drink of water and sneaked back into bed without waking her sister. She lay there in the dark for a long time, thinking about the rag doll before she went back to sleep.

The next morning when she woke up, she thought of the doll again. Then a strange thought occurred to her. What if the doll wasn't for her? It might be for her sister Mary, even if she was older, or maybe for a poor child who didn't have any dolls at all. After all, she did have three little ones, counting the corn husk one. She decided not to say anything to anyone, but to just wait and see.

Christmas was only a week away. Today there would be a Christmas Program at school. Ella had many things to think about, but she did not forget about the doll. At night she tried sneaking downstairs to see if she could watch mother sewing again, but she found only darkness.

Finally, the pies were baked, the goose was stuffed and ready for the oven. Cookies and other sweets were made. Popcorn was strung to hang on the Christmas tree and many bright paper chains were made in red and green. Tomorrow was Christmas. When everyone came downstairs, the tree would be up and decorated, and the presents would be under the tree. Ella would find out for sure about the doll.

*Ella's Stories*

It was hard to go to sleep that night. Ella and Mary were both excited and whispered back and forth until quite late before they both fell asleep.

Early the next morning, Ella was awakened by her little brother Eddie, calling out "wake up everybody! Wake up! It's Christmas morning! It's Christmas morning!" as he ran downstairs.

Ella hopped out of bed and put on her slippers and quickly followed. Father came down right behind her and started a fire in the big wood cook stove so the house would get warm. Soon everyone was there, and father said they could light the candles and look at the beautiful Christmas tree now. They could see all the pretty decorations and the beautiful candles all lit up. Ella had been trying not to peek, but that was really hard not to do, when you are so excited.

Father went to the tree and started handing out presents, he said, "Ella, this has your name on it," as he picked up the most beautiful, yellow haired, pink cheeked, blue dressed rag doll in the whole wide world.

*Ella's Stories*

As he held out the doll to Ella, tears of joy filled her eyes as she said, "Oh thank you father, mother, thank you. This is the most BEAUTIFUL DOLL AND THE BEST CHRISTMAS SURPRISE, EVER…..!"

(I can just see the excitement that Christmas morning as that little boy, my grandfather, Eddie, Shouted Merry Christmas as he came down the stairs. I ran up and down those stairs when I was a little girl, and can see the Christmas tree (in my mind) as it is all lit up in the living room.) The wood cookstove sat in the kitchen in a short pony wall so you could always see what was on the other side, and smell all of the lovely smells. I remember seeing blackberry pies in the pantry just under the stairs.

Grandma Mae

# Yum Yum

It was a lazy warm summer day. Ella was sitting in the shade under the old winter pear tree beside the kitchen window. She was trying to read a book about a Kitten but she was just too sleepy. "Oh," she thought, "summer is such an easy, peaceful time. I have all my work done and I think I shall take a nap. It is so warm."

Just then, Mother came around the corner, calling Ella. "Oh, there you are. I was looking for you. It is too warm to do much cooking on the stove in the kitchen, so I am going to make the apple butter outside in the fireplace out in back of the house, so I won't heat up the house so."

Ella was familiar with this process. When Mother made soap, she always cooked it in a big iron kettle over a big bonfire in the back yard because it smelled so bad while it cooked. Ella usually had to stand there and stir and stir and stir with a very long handled wooden spoon while things cooked in that old kettle.

"Ella," said Mother. "I certainly could use your help just now. I have apples all washed, peeled and cored. They are ready for cooking. I have a fire started and the kettle in place. Will you please help me dump the bowls of apples into the kettle so I won't spill any on the ground and latter will you stir the apple butter for me. It would be a shame for any of that apple butter to scorch. You know how much you like it on fresh homemade bread in the winter time."

Ella was wide awake now. APPLE BUTTER, YUM! YUM! Ella certainly did like it on Mother's fresh bread. She liked it when her older brother John made bread too. He could bake just like Mother. That was probably because mother had taught him how.

Ella knew how hot it would be, stirring the big kettle and that the smoke would get in their eyes. She knew how very tired she would get and how boring it would all seem before she was through. But she also knew how good it would taste next winter and that this was the only chance there was to make the apple butter. Mother had all the apples ready and it was now or never.

"I will help, Mother. I just love apple butter, and on fresh bread, it's the best thing ever!"

(Pioneer families did their best to can and preserve all of the foods they would need during the winter months.)

# Ella Goes away to school

It was graduation time and Ella had just finished the eighth grade and graduated from grade school. Mother had a beautiful new white dress made for her to wear to the ceremony at school. She felt so very grown up.

When they got home that night, Father said he was very proud of her. She always had good grades and had done well in school, "but" he said, you need to go on to high school and I have been thinking about it. Since there is no high school here, just a one room, eight grade, little country school, I think you need to go to Estacada to the high school there. I'll see what I can find out about some place for you to stay and what it will cost. We have a little time yet before school starts, so enjoy your summer and help your mother in the meantime,"

Ella helped her mother and her sister Mary make strawberry jam. She hoed the garden to help the vegetables grow better. She played catch with her younger brother Eddie. She felt very grown up since she had already graduated from the eighth grade. She picked out fabric and shoes from the catalogue for high school in the fall and she went for rides on one of Father's horses whenever she could.

Ella loved to ride and thought how great it would be to take a horse to school with her, in Estacada, but she knew there would be no place to keep one.

About two weeks before time for school to start, Father came in quite pleased, one evening, for supper. "Ella, I think I have good news", he said. "I was talking to the minister from our church and he says the Methodist minister in Estacada is a family man who could use some help and has a spare room. You might be able to stay with

*Ella's Stories*

him and his family and pay your own room and board by working. We must go see him tomorrow."

The next morning Ella got up early and put on her Sunday clothes. She brushed her long red hair and put in a ribbon to match her dress. She even polished her brown leather shoes and thought how glad she had not outgrown them as it was the only pair she had. The catalogue order hadn't come yet.

After breakfast, Father went to the barn to hitch up the buggy for the ride to Estacada. Mary and John were staying home to work and watch out for Eddie. Mother was coming to Estacada with Father and Ella, to see about getting Ella a place to live and registered for school.

It seemed like a very long ride because Ella was very excited. She was wondering what high school would be like. She was thinking about living with a new family and missing Father and Mother. She knew there would be great changes in her life, change was both exciting and scary.

They began to see farms and houses along the road and before long they were in Estacada. It wasn't hard to find the Methodist Church. Father drove right to it. The minister's house was just next door. Father stopped the buggy in front of the house and tied the horse to a post. Then he helped Mother and Ella out of the buggy. They went up the steps to the front door and knocked.

A very nice lady came to the door and asked them to come in and sit down. Father explained why they were there. The lady nodded her head and said to please wait while she called her husband.

In a few minutes she came back with the minister who was all smiles and immediately had to shake Father's hand. They each introduced themselves and sat down again. "My you are just what we have been needing," said the minister. "We would like to have someone give a hand around here, with the housework and cooking and a little baby-sitting once-in- awhile. There is a spare room you could sleep in and you can do your homework on the dining room table. There is pretty good light there. Would that work out for you?" he asked?

Ella looked at her Father and Father looked at Mother, then at Ella. They all nodded. "That would be just fine," said Father. "Ella, it looks like you have a place to stay." We need to go to the high school now and find out when school starts and what you have to bring."

"Fine," said the minister, just let us know when to expect her." "We will," said Father. "Thank you very much. We will let you know."

They left and went by the high school. Ella was able to register and found out what day it started.

Everyone was tired at supper that night, but it was good to know that Ella had a home for the school year.

It was a busy week. The mail order package came, and the seamstress came to stay and made Ella's school clothes and two shirts for Eddie. Mother helped Ella pack her bag (We would call it a suitcase) for the trip to Estacada.

On Sunday before school started, the whole family got into the wagon and took Ella to the minister's house. It was very strange and kind of sad when they said goodbye and left her.

But the minister and his family welcomed her and took her in to dinner. They helped her get settled in her new room and get ready for school the next day.

*Ella's Stories*

Ella made some very good friends at school and the work wasn't too hard. But at the minister's home, it was a different story. Dirty dishes had piled up all day and she was expected to wash them all. The children were not too well behaved, not sweet like her brother Eddie, and they teased her a lot. She seldom got her housework finished before ten p.m. regardless of how hard she tried. Then she still had to do all her homework from school. She had to get up early to help with breakfast and this made her very tired after a few days. But Ella didn't complain. She was paying her own way by working and she loved high school very much. She just wished the minister's wife would allow seconds at mealtime as she did get very hungry.

Things went on without changing for several weeks, but Ella was getting homesick. She was thinking about her family back on the farm. It really wasn't that far away. If you went by the road which went around about, it would be too far to walk but there was a path, straight through the woods, up over a steep hill that would only take three or four hours. She decided to do it! Father could bring her back on Monday morning, in the wagon. She was sure he wouldn't mind.

She began making her plans. She told the minister's wife on Thursday night that she would be gone for the weekend as she wanted to visit her family. She worked extra hard at school so she wouldn't have any homework for the weekend. She packed a little extra in her lunch bag, so she would have a snack after school. (The minister's wife didn't approve of such things as snacks).

Then… she came straight home after school to leave her extra things. She got her sweater, ate her snack and started for the trail through the woods.

Ella was so happy, looking forward to seeing Mother, Father, Mary, John and Eddie. She was humming to herself as she walked right along. She started early enough to make it clear through the woods before dark. She was feeling very brave and she knew there was nothing in the woods to hurt her, but it was kind of dark. The path led between the tall fir trees. There were big clumps of ferns, Rhododendrons and Huckleberry bushes. There were many birds flitting through the treetops. On one tree a small squirrel stopped nibbling on something he held in his paws, scold Ella for walking by his tree. Then she heard

*Ella's Stories*

a rustling in some dry leaves and stopped to see what it was. She stood very still and saw two little rabbits that were playing. "How cute", she thought. "They don't seem to have a care in the world, and neither do I, for the weekend. My homework is caught up and I won't have to do any housework or baby-sitting. Mother will have lots of good food to eat and I can sleep late tomorrow morning."

Ella was daydreaming about her weekend home as she came around a turn in the path…. And what do you think she almost ran straight into? A small black bear! Ella shrieked! The poor little bear stood up on his hind legs and looked very surprised. He snorted and took off as fast as his four little legs could carry him, down the path Ella had just come up. Ella took off running up the path the other way. She ran and ran. Finally, she stopped to catch her breath. She turned and looked back down the path but there was no sign of the bear.

"Well," she thought, "I think it scared the bear as much as it did me and he really wasn't that big of a bear."

Ella slowed down and continued toward home. Within the hour she was out of the woods and on the road. She was very excited and would soon be there.

Eddie was out playing in the front yard and saw her coming. "Mother, Mother", he called "Ella's coming."

*Ella's Stories*

By the time she got to the front door, the whole family was there to meet her. There were many hugs to welcome her home.

The long walk home was well worth it.

Authors note: Ella graduated from the eight-grade in an area called Dover, Oregon, near the homestead of her parents. She went away to high school at age thirteen, to Estacada, Oregon. She never lived at home again. She only lived one school year with the minister's family. Her second, third and fourth years, she lived with Mrs. Heilman was delighted to have Ella in her elegant home and she did everything in her power to spoil Ella, which was much appreciated.

Ella kept in touch with her dear friends from high school. She attended class reunions until she was in her late seventies and her health prevented her from going.

# Stories of Grandfather Alex

# Alex's Christmas Surprise

Alexander was just a little boy who lived in a small house built of stones with a thatched roof. He lived with his mother and father, brothers and sisters. It was about 1870 on the Isle of Shapinsay, in the Orkney Islands just north of the main part of Scotland. He was a happy little boy who would be starting school soon.

Alex liked to watch his mother prepare food for her family. Mother, Mary would build up the fire in the fireplace, then would hang up the great big black kettle on the hook in the fireplace. Mother would add some water and some chunks of mutton to cook, then she would add vegetables and other good spices. His Mother stirred the kettle with a long handled wooden spoon. The food would bubble slowly until the meat was tender and the other vegetables were cooked. When Alexander's father came home, would lift the heavy kettle onto the middle of the table and each of them would pick up their own wooden spoon and all eat out of the big kettle. It was a good time for the family to eat and enjoy each other's company.

When Christmas time came near, father was keeping some secrets. He had something he was doing that we couldn't see. It was very exciting to think of Christmas day approaching.

When Christmas day came, Father said there were special presents. Everyone had to close their eyes and hold out their hands, and into each hand Father placed a brand new, hand carved wooden bowl. Father had been making them as a surprise for his little family. Then he explained that each of them could now have their own bowl of food for themselves to eat with their own spoon. They would no longer have to eat out of the big black kettle. James' family was overjoyed to think

*Ella's Stories*

of Fathers lovely, hand carved gifts. They couldn't help being excited as they waited for Christmas dinner to use their beautiful wooden bowls. What a blessing it was to be a Bews that special Christmas morning.

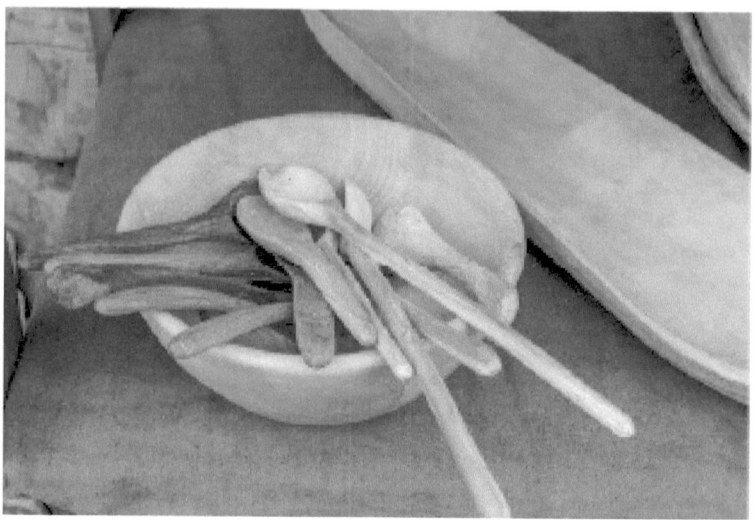

# The Journey

Alexander Bews and Mary Harray both worked in the City of London, England. Alexander drove a hackney cab (a type of horse and buggy, which people hired like a taxi-cab would be hired today).

Mary was an upstairs laundress for a rich family, whose only daughter, a teenager, was dying of consumption, which we now call tuberculosis. The family kept everything scented with strong French perfume to cover the odor of sickness and pending death. Mary had such strong memories of the smell that she could never stand perfume again, and never wore any. It was there in London that Alexander and Mary met and then married. It was around the year 1891. They had a son about 1892, whom they named John Harray Bews.

They had saved enough money for their passage by boat to America, so they went home to Scotland, in the Orkney Isles, to say goodbye to their families and collect young Jimmy. Jimmy (James) was Alex's son by his first marriage. Jimmy's mother had died in childbirth and he had been left with his doting grandparents James and Mary Bews.

James and Mary Drever (Bews) were the parents of eleven children, Alex being number four, he was born in April of 1865. Their youngest child was just a little older than Jimmy, so he fit right into the family. Gramma was heartbroken at the thought of losing her youngest baby and pleaded with Alex and Mary to let Jimmy stay with her. Alex and Mary couldn't stand to see her in so much pain, so they decided to leave Jimmy in Scotland with his grandparents as guardians. (When

Jimmy was 18 years old, his father sent him money to come to America, but he used the money to stay in Scotland and get married instead of traveling to America.)

Alex and Mary Bews bought passage on a cattle boat which was the least expensive way to cross the ocean. Even at that, it cost them over $300 apiece for tickets. They left England from an unknown port, probably in southern England. Later in life Alex remarked that the crossing was one of the worst experiences of his life. The awful smells and rough voyage left a terrible impression on him which he remembered throughout his life. When they entered New York harbor they saw the Statue of Liberty, what an amazing sight.

Alex and Mary with baby John came through Ellis Island as immigrants, when this port of entry was still new. Because they were all in good health, and their papers were all in order, they were passed quickly through the tests performed on new arrivals at Ellis Island. (year 1893). They carried a large pile of luggage and goods to set up their new home in America. A few days after clearing immigration at Ellis Island this Bews family of three, left New York by train for Sacramento California.

The family boarded a train, traveling down the East Coast, across the southern states and up the west coast to Sacramento, California. The trip took about 5 days, they took their own food, buying everything they needed to make healthy sandwiches and large bag of apples. This was the food they had to eat as the food on board the train was terribly expensive. They slept on the train sitting up in their seats, for five days and nights, how uncomfortable that must have been for such a long trip. The immigrants really must have wanted to come to America and start a new life, to go through the many hardships they endured.

Alex had made up his mind as a child to go to America, when the local taxes grew out of hand. Alex had to quit school after 4$^{th}$ grade and work for his father herding sheep, he had a black and white border collie he named Johnny that he taught to help with the sheep. Johnny, his dog, was his friend and companion, they spent every day and each night together.

The government in Scotland changed their laws and had a tax levied on dogs. Alex's father didn't have enough extra money to pay the tax, so instead of paying the tax, Johnny, Alex's dog, was killed because of the law. Alex said he never could be proud of being a Scot again because of the loss of his special friend and companion. When Alex moved to America, he said, "I am very proud of being an American and I'm willing to pay reasonable and fair taxes in this great country."

In America Alex was able to have many dogs throughout his life to care for and help him care for his many animals.

When Alex and Mary, with baby John, who was about a year and a half old, reached Sacramento, they found jobs in a logging camp. Alex worked felling trees and Mary made three enormous meals each day for the big hungry loggers. They both worked hard as crew for the logging camp in Sacramento for about a year. During that year baby Mary Jane was born.

When the family had saved enough money to buy a wagon, team of horses, supplies and a little to spare, they quit their jobs, packed up the kids and headed north for Oregon. They had heard about how great the land in Oregon was for farming. The Bews family could homestead for free if they were willing to follow the government rules and put work into the land and in building a home. Alex and Mary were willing to work hard for a home in this new country of America.

The road leading north was lonely, but they didn't mind. They were on their way to their own property and a chance to have their

## Ella's Stories

own home. The wagon was able to travel just a few miles a day; dust, heat and the bumpy ride, were very exhausting but their spirits were high and there was joy in their hearts. This was America and they were part of a great adventure.

As they were traveling through what was called Dry Lakes, in Northern California, they came to a lonesome ranch, miles away from anyone else. The ranch looked like a good place to spend the night. It should be safe and there should be water for the animals and more to fill the water barrels on the back of the wagon. Mary was excited about the chance to have other people to talk to. It turned out that they were right. The family was very glad to have visitors, in fact, so very glad that they convinced them to stay several days so the ladies could talk and Mary could tell all the latest news from Sacramento and show the lady of the ranch the magazines she had bought in New York city, before she got on the train. The magazines she bought had all of the latest fashions about what women should wear and ideas for decorating your new home. In fact, Mary left those magazines with the lady when it was time to leave… they meant that much to her. The lady had been raised in Boston society and was terribly lonely out in northern California with nobody but ranch hands to talk to. She cried when her new friend Mary left and said she never would forget her.

When she was older, she told a neighbor girl (yes, she finally had neighbors) about the dear little Scottish lady that had been traveling through, stayed to visit and had left the precious fashion magazines with her. (Mary Kathleen, Mary's granddaughter, lived next door to this woman in Klamath Falls, when her children were little and heard stories about her own grandmother and her travels.)

After Alex and Mary left Dry Lakes, the map became somewhat confusing and they took a wrong turn. It seemed longer than they figured to the next point on the map, and sure enough, they ended up in Lakeview, Oregon instead of Klamath Falls. It took precious time for them to backtrack, and six very, very stressful weeks to get back on the correct route. (That route would eventually become the present highway 97, going through central Oregon). Alex, Mary and their family were blessed that the weather held out and they got on the correct road again. They had so much to do when they arrived in Beaverton including building a home to live in before winter was upon them. God was truly watching out for them as their trip really went smoothly the rest of the way. They were awe struck as they came on the scenery of central Oregon.

It was at the Crooked River crossing that Alexander and Mary Bews met another family. They were delighted to find another couple that were headed for the area around Portland, intending to homestead there also. The families quickly decided to travel together. Alexander was heard to say later that when they came to the Crooked River Gorge, he couldn't believe what he saw! A crack in the earth of such magnitude that it looked impossible to cross. However, true to the strength and tenacity of the pioneering spirit, a way was found down one side and up the other with a river to ford in the bottom. Nothing in their previous experiences had prepared them for what they found. Nothing of this sort existed in Scotland where they had come from.

The two families were headed up the south slopes of Mt. Hood. The trees were big and beautiful and promised a good life and prosperity for both couples. As they made their way over the pass and looked at the north slope of the mountain, they couldn't believe the beauty, and the great expanse of forest and land. The poor couples were appalled at the drop of elevation and the terrible steep slope that they would have to traverse.

Even though they had heard about this steep slope it just didn't seem possible. Because they came from their homeland in Shapinsay, a seven-mile long island in the Orkneys, just north of mainland Scotland, they could never have imagined the drop off that lay ahead. Both families did as they had been told to do by those who had marked their maps for them. They each cut down a large tree and securely fastened them to the back of their wagons to act as a drag brake to slow their decent down the part of the trail called the Laurel chute, it is said that there are places in the trail that are as much as 60% grade. The men unhitched the teams and took off all harnesses. I'm sure they must have asked God for help as this was an awfully scary thing to do after they had come so far. Next, they led the horses over the edge to find their own way down. When the horses were safe, they pushed the first wagon over the edge and watched it careen crazily to the

*Ella's Stories*

bottom, then they pushed the second wagon. Alex and Mary were so thankful that their wagon rolled down safely. They watched in horror as their new friends' wagon went part way down and then rolled over and over, destroying the wagon and almost everything in it. When the wagons had quit moving it was safe for the people to start hiking down the hill. It is at a time like this that friends show their true value. By working together both families stayed safe and made it to their destination to begin building their new lives. (Laurel grade is still on the southern slopes of Mt. Hood and still occasionally claims a vehicle trying to descend the steep grade.)

These brave and courageous souls and many others just like them, from countries all over the world, are what America is built from. They believed in God's love and grace, and a man's right to be free to work, worship and live in peace, and that their neighbor, no matter where they came from had the same rights as they did, themselves.

The Bews family arrived at their destination in Beaverton on their land grant (homestead claim) before Eleanor was born in 1898.

Alexander's hope to establish a working farm was a disappointment due to the poor quality of soil on this homestead. The Beaverton claim was sold a short time later. They located a short distance away in Farmington and then they moved to Laurel, still searching for the right soil. Son, William Edwin, was born in Laurel, September 8, 1901. Alexander was still not satisfied with the quality of this soil either. He heard of a claim in Dover 55 to 60 miles away, that was mostly logged, and traveled several weeks to go to the claim and buy it. Then came the task of moving all of their belongings to the new home along with his growing family. Grandfather did not have quite enough money to purchase the land outright so needed to pay more the next year. (Please read the story of Ella's Big Adventure)

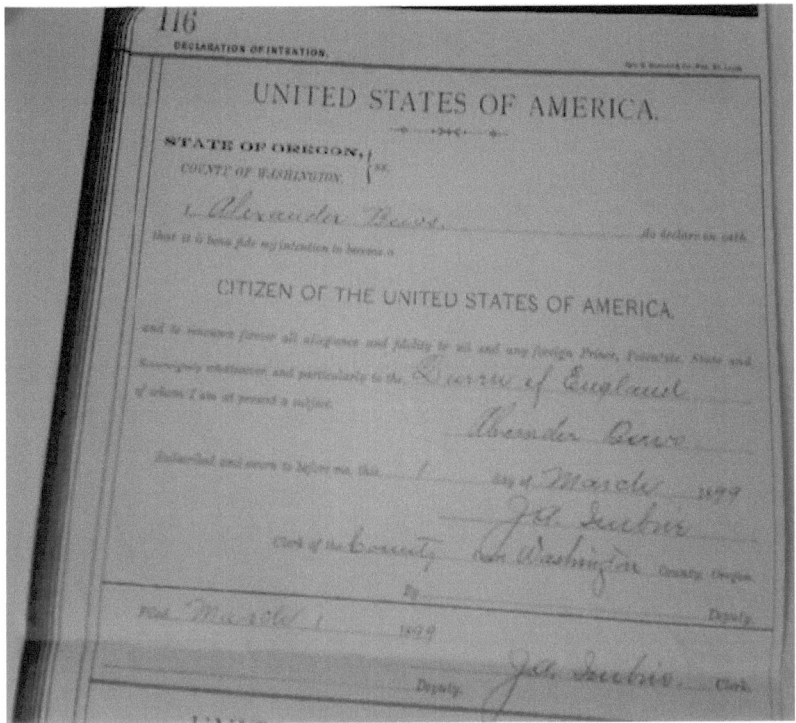

The first crops were most likely vegetables for the family table, with hay and grain to sell. They raised enough beets, beans, corn, squash, cabbage and turnips to fill their root cellar. Most likely they traded with the neighbors for berries.

Dairy farming seemed to be more lucrative than just raising crops. Alexander, therefore found it necessary to adjust his thinking and planted pasture for cattle and sheep to graze. Eventually the farm supported 100 head of fine Brown Swiss dairy stock. Alexander built a barn and later a milking facility, after his home was established. Several years went by with Alexander and Mary comfortably successful as dairy farmers. Alex's dairy stock of choice was the gentle brown swiss cows.

****That barn was re-roofed when Mary Kathleen was a young girl, probably around 1940. Her grandfather Alexander showed her how to split shakes and she got to make some of the shakes! She didn't think her shakes were very good, but grandpa said they were sure good enough, and he used every one of the shakes.***

There was a story told about Alexander Bews, when he was about 16 years old, back in Scotland. Alex and a few of his friends took on a Halloween prank to fix a grumpy neighbor that was always hassling the boys. They crept onto his place in the night, dismantled his new farm wagon and reassembled it on the roof of his barn. The rest of the story is missing. I bet everyone got a good laugh out of that prank.

Alex and Mary Bews had four children, John Harray, born in England. Mary Jane born in Sacramento, California, on the way to Oregon. Eleanor Isabel, born in Beaverton and Edwin William, born in Laurel.

John Harray, the young son who came to America with his mom and dad joined the army at the beginning of World War 1, spending most of his army life in France. After the war John moved to Soda Springs, Idaho where he met and married Frances Rudd. They operated a farm there just outside of Soda Spring. John lived in Idaho all of his adult life. John and his wife Francis never had children of their own, but they adopted a son Harold Michael who had been a child who was abandoned.

Eleanor Isabel, one of Alexander and Mary's children, went to high school in Estacada. Estacada was approximately 10 miles from the home place, too far to drive to every day. (Please see our story Ella goes away to school)

After Eleanor graduated from High School in 1916, she taught school for one year at the Dover school, she then went to school in Portland to get additional schooling as a secretary. When she arrived in Portland, she stayed for a short time with Lucille Williams and later found a room in a boarding house just a few blocks from downtown Portland. The boarding house was operated by Nettie Hicks, George Hicks mother. Eleanor had been briefly acquainted with the Hicks family in Estacada. (Later Eleanor married George Hicks).

Several years after Eleanor graduated from High School, Alex and Mary left the place in Dover for Eddie to run and traveled to Soda Springs, Idaho, where they established a new farm. Eddie later moved to Soda Springs to be near his parents leaving the home place empty for a few years. Grandpa Alex and Grandmother Mary moved back to the home place in the early to mid- 1930's.

During the time her parents lived in Soda Springs, Eleanor made several trips by train to see the family. The fare was inexpensive, and it gave her a chance to spend an occasional weekend with her parents. On one of those weekend trips, there was a train wreck and Eleanor was knocked unconscious. When she came to with a sheet over her, she thought she was dead. Then someone spoke to her. Other than a bump on the head she was all right. What a story to remember.

Eddie was a well-known member of the Bews family, at one time he received a gift of a retired polo pony from the chief of the Warm Springs Indian tribe.

When son, Edwin and his wife Pauline took over the place in Dover, they were well known, not only for their fine dairy farm, but as a secure home for troubled children, as foster parents.

Some of us forget these facts of how our families immigrated to America. We get off track in our thinking, but every year we celebrate the birthday of this country and why this country was started and get back on track. No wonder America is the greatest country in the world!

Grandfather Alexander and Grandmother Mary

www.ingramcontent.com/pod-product-compliance
Ingram Content Group UK Ltd.
Pitfield, Milton Keynes, MK11 3LW, UK
UKHW041956230426
12048UKWH00008B/376